Printed by Author In Me in the United Kingdom
Design Illustration: Ekta Bajaj
Creative concept : Author In Me

This edition has been published by Author In Me Ltd.

Published in the UK
www.authorinme.com

YOUNG VOICES

Written by
Deeva Karnani Shah
13 years old

RESURGENCE

Content

Chapter 1

Task

AUGUST 3089

Astrid refreshed his computer screen, the soft glow casting a bluish hue on his intense face. He stared blankly at the screen, the cursor blinking in rhythm with his thoughts. The assignment, a digital puzzle of words and ideas, seemed to mock him with its complexity

As he stared blankly at the screen, his fingers hovered momentarily over the keyboard, suspended in a delicate balance between ideas and action.

Astrid's brow furrowed as he tried to unravel the web of mathematical concepts before him. Each equation felt like a tangled thread in a vast, intricate tapestry. He had always prided himself on his analytical mind, but this assignment was pushing the limits of his intellect.

With a sigh of frustration, he leaned back in his chair, rubbing his temples to alleviate the growing headache. The weight of the task seemed to bear down on him, and self-doubt crept in. Maybe he wasn't as capable as he thought. Perhaps he had bitten off more than he could chew.

While Astrid was lost in his own
thoughts, he heard a faint sound from
the next room. It was his mother's
voice, and it sounded unusually
vulnerable. Astrid strained his ears to
listen more closely, his concerns about
the assignment momentarily pushed
aside.

"...I told you, I can't do this
anymore," Emily's voice trembled as
she spoke on the phone. "You can't
keep threatening me like this. I know
you have plans to demote me as an
undergrounder if I don't follow your
instructions, but I don't care!"

Astrid's heart skipped a beat. His mother's voice had never sounded like this before. The urgency in her tone sent a shiver down his spine. He had to find out what was happening. Without hesitation, he pushed his chair back and left his homework behind, determined to investigate the mysterious conversation taking place in just a room away.

Astrid quietly made his way to the living room, where he found his mother seated on the couch with her phone pressed to her ear. Her face was etched with worry, her eyes darting around the room as if she expected someone to burst through the door at any moment.

"Mom," Astrid whispered, his voice laced with concern as he approached her.

Emily jumped at the sound of his voice, quickly ending the call and placing her phone on the coffee table. She tried to put on a reassuring smile but couldn't quite hide the fear in her eyes.

"Astrid, what are you doing here?" she asked, attempting to sound casual.

Astrid knelt beside her; his gaze locked onto hers. "I overheard your conversation. Are you okay? Who was that on the phone?"

Emily hesitated for a moment, her lips trembling. She glanced around the room nervously before finally speaking, "Astrid, it's nothing. Just some work-related issues. You don't need to worry."

But Astrid could sense that something was seriously wrong. He had never seen his mother in such an apprehensive and fearful state, and her explanation didn't sit well with him. "Mom, please," he implored, "I heard you say something about threats. Is someone bothering you? You can trust me."

"Astrid, don't worry about it. It's nothing."

Astrid returned to his room and sat hunched over his keyboard; his eyes fixed to the screen. Unable to focus on his assignment, he began to type out a plan, determined to uncover the secrets that his mother was hiding and protect her at all costs.

The gentle glow of numerous computers' displays cast unsettling shadows across Astrid's face as he sat in his poorly illuminated space.

Lines of code scrolled rapidly on one screen, while on another, he manipulated virtual defences like a digital puppeteer. At the tender age of fifteen, he was already a prodigious hacker, known only by his online alias, "Cipher." His reputation within the underground hacking community was formidable. Whispers of his exploits reverberated through the encrypted forums and darknet channels where hackers congregated.

His playground was the digital world, which he manoeuvred with the skill of a pro. His abilities went far beyond simple mischief or curiosity.

While his classmates struggled
with their schoolwork, Astrid was
perfecting the skill of getting over
firewalls, breaking encryptions, and
erasing any digital traces.

The underground hacking
community had always been a
clandestine world, hidden from the
prying eyes of the overgrounder
authorities. It was a place where the
Overgrounders' strict control over
information could be subverted, if only
temporarily.

Astrid revelled in this subversive
world. It had all started with an
innocuous curiosity, a desire to
understand the world beyond

the curated narratives of the Overgrounders. Astrid had stumbled upon a group of like-minded individuals who shared his thirst for knowledge and truth — the Undergrounders, who were a loose collective of hackers, activists, and rebels.

The division between Overgrounders and Undergrounders had deep historical roots, dating back to the tumultuous period known as 'The Great Divide.' In the early 22nd century, society had split into two factions—the Overgrounders and Undergrounders.

As Astrid delved deeper into the world of hacking, he learned about the origins of this division. The Overgrounders had gained power through technological advancements and manipulation. With their superior technology, wealth, and influence, they became leaders of the society.

Those who did not support unethical AI use were labelled as undergrounders. These individuals were stripped of their high-ranking roles, lost their identity rights, and were prohibited from contributing to the society. They weren't even considered citizens in the eyes of the world. The wilderness was the only safe heaven left for them, and they relied on their hacking skills to fight back against false information, wrongdoings, and injustices caused by those in power.

These Undergrounders weren't allowed in the tech advanced cities that were guarded by robotic security forces. Many tried to invade but never succeeded. It was impossible to evade the AI-powered security forces; all they needed to do was take one look into a person's eyes to verify their identity. These apathetic monsters were programmed to shoot any

Undergrounders on sight.

During this time, the underground hacking community flourished, its members using their digital prowess to expose the corruption and deception of the Overgrounders. Astrid, a young prodigy with an insatiable appetite for AI and technology joined them.

***

As Astrid sat in his room that night, his thoughts returned to his mother and the cryptic phone call he had overheard earlier. The memories of his hacking days and the battle between the Overgrounders and Undergrounders seemed irrelevant now.

Something was bothering him, something that threatened his family, and he couldn't ignore it.

Chapter-2

Quest

"I need to find the people who have divided the human race into Overgrounders and Undergrounders," Astrid mumbled firmly.

With deft keystrokes, Astrid navigated through the layers of digital

security of the Overgrounder's
headquarters, bypassing firewalls
and encryption protocols. His
determination to save his mother
and unravel the mystery behind the
threats propelled him forward as he
delved into the government's systems,
seeking to uncover the data that
created the big divide in the human
race — the identity of the threatener,
and any clues that might lead him to
a way to protect his loved ones.

When he was about to open the
file with the list of Overgrounders
who were next to be robbed off their
identity, another firewall appeared.
He felt a flicker of familiarity.

There was something about the code structure that resonated with him. He paused; his fingers hovered over the keyboard with a sense of disbelief washing all over him.

He recognised the code as he knew the author. The shock consumed him as he traced the lines back to their originator. The author of the code had to be none other than his long-lost frenemy, Hikaru.

Astrid and Hikaru shared a deep friendship when Hikaru was an Overgrounder, but rivalry also thrived between them. Astrid could never breach the impenetrable firewalls crafted by Hikaru.

His gaze moved around, looking for familiar and unfamiliar answers. His beating heart was spurred by curiosity as he wondered how Hikaru was involved in this complex network of government secrets.Hikaru is an Undergrounder, and he is helping Overgrounders?

What's going on? Astrid pondered aloud, "Where could Hikaru be? What secrets does he hold? How can I break through this stubborn firewall?" Then, he muttered to himself, "I need to track down Hikaru to find the answers and break the firewall."

He remembered about a place where hackers gathered to exchange information and boast about their skills.

Astrid's heart raced as he followed the route to the secret hacker hangout. He finally arrived at a secret computer lab with dim lighting. The room was filled with an array of monitors casting an eerie glow, each screen displaying lines of code and intricate digital patterns. It was a place where innumerable relationships and secrets had been forged, a sanctuary for hackers. He was nervous. As he entered the secret room, the sound of conversations and keyboard clicks became louder, signalling his arrival at this hidden digital spot.

Astrid took a deep breath, his eyes scanning the room, searching for any sign of Hikaru in the dark glare of the monitors. Determined to learn the truth, he typed in a secret signal—a coded message on his wristwatch and sent it to all the hackers sitting in the room. But he knew only Hikaru would recognise it if he received it. It was a gamble, a way to confirm whether his old friend was indeed behind the mysterious coding style he had encountered.

With a sense of anticipation and tension in the air, Astrid sent the message, hoping for a response that would provide the answers he sought.

His eyes scanned the room like a programmed robot. A beep on his wristwatch interrupted his attention.

Is it Hikaru? He opened the message to confirm.

Chapter 3

Plan

Yes!

Astrid jumped with joy. He scanned the room again and followed the direction of the signal. Sitting at a desk in the corner of the room, bathed in the eerie blue light of the monitor was Hikaru.

Astrid took a tentative step forward, the sound of his own breath echoed in his ears. He watched as Hikaru's fingers danced across the keyboard, effortlessly manipulating the digital realm.

As if sensing Astrid's presence, Hikaru glanced up. A mixture of surprise and nostalgia emerged across his face.

He greeted Astrid with a small smile, tugging at the corners of his lips.

Astrid returned the smile, relief and curiosity mingling in his expression.

"Hikaru, it's been years. I never thought I'd see you here of all places."

Hikaru chuckled, a familiar glint in his eyes. "You know how it is, Astrid. Once a hacker, always a hacker. What brings you back to this world?"

Astrid hesitated for a moment, his gaze shifting to the monitors that surrounded them.

"I... I need answers, Hikaru. Something's happened — involving the government and my mother. They are demoting my mum to an Undergrounder and threatening her. You know my mum has always been a trustworthy counsellor of Government officials. She was the first lady who turned emotionless robots into kind and caring health workers. She is the one who trained robots to become expert doctors. I don't understand why the government officials are planning to demote her. Why are they threatening her? What do they want from her? I need answers."

"I am aware the government has some sinister plans, Astrid. They're orchestrating killings to maintain their control and suppress any dissent. They are transforming kind and friendly robots into ruthless killers. They want to create fear and chaos, to maintain their oppressive measures and tighten their grip on power."

Astrid's eyes widened in shock and disbelief. "But... why? How could they do such a thing? What purpose does it serve?"

Astrid's voice quivered as he revealed the next part, the part that hit closest to home. "Hikaru, they have her captive, although she didn't tell me, they're forcing my mother to carry out some sinister plans."

Hikaru's brows furrowed deeply, a sharp crease forming between them. His eyes narrowed. However, the slight downturn of the corners of his mouth and the tension in his jawline revealed a hint of underlying worry.

"No, Astrid, this can't be true. Your mother, she's... she's like family to me too. We have to do something. I am not involved in programming those robots. They have hired me to create some very specific firewalls so that no one could hack their system, but you know, we can't let them continue this reign of terror. I have access to various systems for Overgrounders since I created them whilst working for them. I know how to corrupt those systems. But to do so, we need to reach the AI vault. They hired me because they knew no one could match my programming skills, but maybe they didn't realise that if I can create something, I can also easily break it if needed."

A determined fire ignited within Astrid's eyes as he nodded. "You're right, Hikaru. We can't stand idly by while innocent lives are taken and our loved ones are used as pawns. We need to expose the government's true face, their corruption, and manipulation of the system."

Astrid's mind raced, searching for a way to bring down the oppressive regime and liberate his mother from their clutches.

"We have to find the way to reach the AI vault," Hikaru declared, his voice firm.

Astrid nodded, a glimmer of hope returning to his eyes. "We'll need help, Hikaru. Trustworthy allies who share our vision of a just and free society. Together, we'll fight back, not just for my mother, but for everyone who has suffered under their tyranny."

Astrid's eyes shone with an inner fire as he looked at Hikaru. "We can't let fear hold us back," he said firmly.

Hikaru nodded; his expression resolute.

***

Astrid and Hikaru were determined to find the AI vault, the key to unravelling the government's secrets and exposing their corruption. They knew it wouldn't be easy, but they were up for the challenge.

They started by scouring the darkest corners of the dark web, where rumours of the AI vault's location occasionally surfaced. They followed leads, traded favours, and hacked into encrypted forums, all while keeping their identities hidden.

As days passed, they gathered fragmented information that pointed towards a remote and well-guarded facility in a desolate region. Its exact coordinates remained elusive, but Astrid knew he and Hikaru were getting closer.

Exactly one week later, back in hacker's hangout, Astrid's fingers hovered over the keyboard, uncertainty etched into his furrowed brow. "Hikaru, look at this. It's a message from an anonymous source, and it hints at a hidden server within the government's network."

Hikaru leaned in closer, his eyes narrowing as he absorbed the message.

The gravity of the situation settled upon his shoulders, a mix of concern and determination reflected in the lines on his face. "This could be it, Astrid. The key to everything we've been searching for."

With their hacking skills honed to perfection, they began their mission. They typed quickly, breaking through security measures. The room was filled with the rhythmic clattering of keys.

They moved so quickly; it was like they were invisible online. They broke through all the computer's security, like kids beating a hard video game level.

The room felt tense as they got
closer to their goal. They were both so
focused; you could hear the computers
buzzing.

Finally, they made it to the secret
place they were looking for. Hikaru
looked at Astrid, his face was beaming
with a blend of excitement and
concern. "We did it."

It contained a treasure trove of
classified information, including the
coordinates of the AI vault. Astrid's
heart raced as he confirmed the
location.

"We've found it, Hikaru," Astrid
whispered. "The AI vault's coordinates

are here. We know where it is."

Hikaru's voice crackled with enthusiasm. "Excellent work, Astrid. Now, we must plan our next move carefully. We can't afford to make any mistakes."

With the location of the AI vault in their possession, Astrid felt that they were one step closer to exposing the government's secrets and bringing an end to their oppressive regime.

Chapter 4

Danger

The dawn was breaking, casting a soft orange hue across the city. A government building, massive and imposing, stood tall against the horizon. Its reflective windows shimmered in the early morning sun, giving nothing away about the secrets that lay within. Surprisingly, there were no guards near the premises.

Hidden in the shadow of a nearby alley, Astrid stood with Hikaru. He saw Hikaru adjust the straps of his backpack, pulling out a map.

"This is the building's blueprint, "Hikaru whispered, laying it out for Astrid to see.

"The AI vault is here, deep inside, in the basement. We don't know whom we have to face and fight. I've heard someone mighty guards the vault — Metal Man."

Astrid's eyes widened, having heard tales of the Metal Man, an AI robot with formidable strength and advanced sensors.

"We need a strategy. I've got a few smoke bombs and some tech that might disrupt its sensors, at least temporarily."

Hikaru nodded. It seemed to Astrid that Hikaru appreciated his foresight.

"Perfect. While you create a diversion, I'll try to sneak up from behind and disable whatever comes at us. But remember, time is of the essence. We need to get in and out before security guards arrive."

***

After entering the building, Astrid crouched for a moment. He indicated to Hikaru to do the same. They needed to go over every detail of their plan, ensuring that nothing was overlooked. Astrid saw the intensity in Hikaru's eyes. It spoke volumes as it mirrored the understanding of the dangerous path they had chosen.

Suddenly, a mechanical hum echoed through the air. Astrid peeked around the corner and saw something unprecedented.

Taking a deep breath, Astrid whispered, "Ready?"

Hikaru nodded. He seemed to Astrid to be steeling himself. "Let's do this."

As they stealthily made their way through the building's dimly lit corridors, the faint hum of electricity and the soft whir of machinery filled the air. The government had spared no expense in safeguarding its most classified information, and the security measures were evident.

Astrid saw a series of advanced security robots, their sleek metallic bodies patrolling the hallways with impeccable efficiency. These were not the clumsy automatons of the past but highly advanced machines, equipped with a variety of defensive mechanisms.

Astrid reminded himself that they had planned it well.

It would all go as per their strategy. And so, it did. In a meticulously choreographed dance of precision and timing, they used their combined skills to disarm the robots. The giant watches on their wrists provided all the information they needed. Tiny computers that they carried in their pockets were their weapons. Hikaru,

with his unparalleled knowledge
of coding, infiltrated the robots'
programming, causing them to
fall into a temporary state of
hibernation.

Astrid, on the other hand, relied
on his physical prowess to swiftly
and silently disable the robots by
switching off the power button that
was fixed on the centre of their chest,
putting them to deep hibernation.
He was gratified that their teamwork
had been flawless, and they had left
a trail of incapacitated guardians in
their wake.

As they ventured deeper into the heart
of the building, a palpable sense of
tension hung in the air. Astrid knew
their ultimate challenge lay ahead —
guarding the main server room. The
room was rumoured impenetrable,
and the man who protected it was
an enigma. The building itself was a
looming fortress of steel and glass, its
imposing façade concealing the secrets
that lay within.

At last, their formidable enemy
stood before them—a metallic figure
with a shiny metal prosthetic hand
of iron glinted in the dim light. He
towered over them menacingly.

Astrid watched as the iron-handed figure, Metal Man, moved forward with calculated steps. Metal Man's footsteps were louder than thunder in a valley. The clank of his heavy boots against the floor moved closer. The growl of his voice, deep and droning, issued a challenge. His words were spoken in a cryptic language. Astrid couldn't help but be horrified by the sight of the prosthetic metal, crafted into the shape of a giant hand.

The Metal Man fixed his attention on Astrid, his intentions clear, to cripple Astrid with its mighty hand.

Astrid clenched his fists, determination burning in his eyes. He couldn't allow Metal Man to thwart their mission.

Metal Man swung his prosthetic hand with devastating force, but Astrid's quick reflexes saved him from a lethal blow. The metallic clang of Metal Man's prosthetic served as a powerful shield, deflecting Astrid's blows with resounding force. His punches were powerful, and the impact sent shockwaves through Astrid's body.

Undeterred, Astrid shifted tactics, relying on his agility to evade Metal

Man's brutal attacks. With a swift and well-placed kick, he made the iron figure tumble. In that crucial moment, Astrid seized the opportunity. His quick thinking led him to disable a critical component of Metal Man's prosthetic. With a precise strike, he disconnected a crucial wire, leaving Metal Man incapacitated and vulnerable.

Astrid momentarily breathed a sigh of relief as Metal Man's main prosthetic lay incapacitated. But his relief was short-lived. From the torso of Metal Man, a swarm of robotic arms began to emerge, each one as menacing as the primary limb. Like a sea anemone, they sprouted from every conceivable angle, each limb primed for attack. The room echoed with the sounds of whirring machinery as the arms waved menacingly.

"Didn't see that coming," whispered Hikaru, a hint of panic evident in his voice.

Astrid, gripping a fallen rod, tried to fend off the approaching limbs, but they seemed almost endless in number. The mechanical limbs were adept, some trying to grab and immobilise while others sought to strike with lethal force.

Hikaru quickly pulled out a small device. Astrid saw that he was probably aiming to send a coded disruption signal to the arms. As he keyed in a rapid sequence, a handful of arms retracted, but the majority remained relentless.

"Oh dear," said Hikaru, 'Each arm belongs to a group that is independently programmed, making them immune to a single overriding command.'

Astrid panicked as their combined efforts seemed almost futile as they found themselves overwhelmed, dodging and parrying the ceaseless barrage. Each arm appeared to have its own style of combat, making them unpredictable and challenging to combat. Some arms lunged like snakes, while others swung like hammers, and some even fired small projectiles.

"We need a plan," Astrid shouted amidst the chaos, his voice hoarse from the exertion. "These things are not going to let up!"

Hikaru, waved his hand and pointed, directing Astrid towards a nearby electrical panel. "If we can overload the circuits, we might be able to sort out these arms!"

Both of them fought their way to the panel, and Hikaru began tampering with the wires. Astrid saw as Hikaru connected several circuits; the room lit up with sparks. Astrid, in the meantime, provided a barrier against the oncoming limbs, using his rod to fend them off as best he could.

But as the seconds ticked by, more arms continued to spawn. Astrid realised they were cornered, their backs pressed against the wall, and the barrage of robotic limbs closing in.

"We need more time," Hikaru murmured, beads of sweat forming on his forehead.

Just then, Bang! And the panel blew up.

Locking eyes for a split second, Astrid understood. They had disarmed the metallic giant for at least few minutes. They sprinted towards a nearby service exit.

After what felt like an eternity, Astrid found shelter in a shadowy cabin and Hikaru was right beside him.

Astrid heard their ragged breaths

and his body ached from the
relentless assault.

"We are nearly there," Hikaru
muttered, his voice tinged with relief.

"But where is the AI vault?" Astrid
responded grimly; uncertainty
clouded his mind.

The AI vault remained elusive,
but Astrid's determination was
undaunted.

Chapter 5

Pursuit

With the rumbling noise of the machineries as a backdrop, Astrid and Hikaru found a secluded corner in the building's atrium. The ornate marble walls stood in stark contrast to the world outside, reminding Astrid of the regime's opulence built on deceit. Hikaru began, "You saw how powerful Metal Man was. We wouldn't have gotten far if we had to go head-to-head with him."

Astrid nodded, rubbing his temple, "You're right. I am glad we blew the panel and it worked. It was a lucky escape, I must say!"

Hikaru paused. He seemed to be thinking, "Remember, everything that emerges from technology has a code. If Metal Man is operating based on some AI integration, there's a central coding system directing him."

Astrid's eyes lit up, "You're suggesting we hack him?"

"In a way," Hikaru said, "but not remotely. We have heard about his "heart" right? This central processor or energy source that's located in the centre of his stomach. That's our target."

Astrid thought for a moment. "If we change the heart's colour from red to blue, it might shift his operating protocol.

Let's try this specially designed electromagnetic pulse device. I am sure it would alter the heart's frequency, switching it from aggressive to passive." He pulled a tiny torch from his backpack.

Astrid exchanged a glance with Hikaru. He saw that Hikaru understood the risks, but also understood that this might be their only chance.

As Astrid prepared to execute their audacious plan, they left their secluded corner and ventured deeper into the government building.

The most challenging obstacle they faced came when they entered a narrow corridor with no apparent exit. Behind them, a seemingly endless horde of robotic limbs emerged, pursuing them relentlessly. The limbs moved with the precision of a well-coordinated swarm, eager to thwart their progress.

In that crucial moment, Hikaru seized the opportunity. Astrid saw how he activated the electromagnetic pulse device they had prepared, directing its energy toward Metal Man's central 'heart.' A surge of blue energy enveloped the heart, altering its frequency from aggressive to passive.

Metal Man staggered, his movements slowing down as the electromagnetic pulse device took effect. The menacing clang of his prosthetic hand became less formidable, and his once-powerful strikes lost their intensity.

His commanding voice mellowed down. Then something incredible happened: the silver giant, in front of them, began to shrink, transforming into a door. Astrid was astounded when they realised their risky plan had worked! As they opened the door, a brightly lit path stretched out ahead of them, leading to the most secure vault.

The vault they sought was the epicentre of the government's deepest secrets, and reaching it was their ultimate goal. The narrow corridor had led them to a colossal chamber, that was both awe-inspiring and intimidating.

The vault was an imposing structure, its entrance a massive door made of reinforced steel. It stood as a sentinel, guarding the government's most closely held information. The room itself was vast, with towering shelves lining the walls, each holding rows upon rows of secure data storage units.

As Astrid and Hikaru entered the vault, Astrid couldn't help but be overwhelmed by the sheer magnitude of the information contained within. The air was cool and dry, filled with the faint hum of countless machines processing and safeguarding classified data.

He knew they had to move quickly, for the clock was ticking. The vault door was timed.

"We have only 10 minutes to execute our plan," Astrid said. His voice was laced with panic.

"I need to identify the master computer that stored all the data," Hikaru replied.

It was a daunting task. Astrid

hoped their keen hacker instincts would guide them.

Astrid, with his experience as a hacker prodigy, scanned the room, his eyes darting from server to server.

"I think I have found it," he shouted.

It was a server unit positioned at the centre of the room, slightly larger and more imposing than the others. It had an intricate web of cables connecting it to various terminals, indicating its significance.

Hikaru indicated to Astrid that the server unit displayed a holographic interface that pulsed with an ominous red hue. Astrid knew it was a telltale sign. This was the heart of the government's malicious operations — the hub through which all their deceitful schemes were deployed.

With firm determination Astrid signalled to Hikaru to move towards the central server. He knew that accessing it would be their ticket to remove the boundaries between the Overground and Underground divide. Time was running out.

As Hikaru began hacking into the central server, his fingers dancing across the keyboard with precision, Astrid watched their surroundings, ready to defend their position from any threats that might emerge. The countdown to revealing the government's secrets had begun, and the fate of their world hung in the balance.

With each passing second, the digital fortress protecting the government's secrets crumbled. Astrid was so proud of their expertise.

His fingers moved swiftly, deleting the database that demarcated Undergrounders and Overgrounders. He fed the data into the system that displayed all the government's treacheries, lies, and manipulations for the public to see.

As he was about to finalise his work, Hikaru abruptly whispered, "We have company."

In the dim light, the silhouette of Metal Man was unmistakable. The hulking figure approached, and the metallic hue of his iron hand glinted threateningly. To their surprise, the Metal Man turned into a kind soul. So, the code had worked, he was not aggressive anymore.

Just then, Astrid's phone rang. The familiar voice on the other end caused his heart to skip a beat. "Mom!" he exclaimed. He stepped aside from his workstation, desperate to hear her voice.

The voice on the other end trembled with emotion. "Astrid, it's me, your mother."

Tears welled up in Astrid's eyes as he choked back his emotions. "Mom, are you okay?"

"Yes, Astrid," his mother answered.

"Even though I'm in hiding, I had to let you know that I'm safe."

Astrid's heart leaped with happiness. He disconnected the phone and returned to his workstation. He finished eradicating the false information while wiping away his emotions. Then he took it out and put the truth in its place — evidence of the oppression, corruption, and lies of the government.

Astrid had a great sense of accomplishment as he typed the last few letters. The task was finished. The public would finally learn the truth because the regime's hold on power had been destroyed.

He turned to face Hikaru. "It's finished," he declared with a jubilant grin. Their lies have been removed from the system."

"We have 90 seconds left, Let's run before the vault door closes," Hikaru yelled.

"May I help?" The Metal Man asked in a gentle polite voice.

"No, thanks. You look after yourself." They laughed in chorus.

They rushed through the secret tunnels, leaving the government's database in shambles. As they stepped outside, the sun was just starting to rise, and their city was experiencing the dawn of a new day.

Astrid couldn't help but feel hopeful and upbeat as they joined the throngs of people on the streets. The regime's hold on the city was eroding as the truth was being made public. Once ruthless, security guards were transformed into gentle guides. There were no barriers that demarcated the Overgrounder AI advanced cities and underground wilderness.

Astrid raised his head to observe the city being illuminated by the morning sun. They had achieved their objective

All's well that ends well! Astrid's mother was safe, the regime's lies had been exposed, the two societies were intermingled and he was reunited with his friend Hikaru forever.

The End.

About the Author

Profile

Deeva Karnani Shah is on a mission to inspire young children to write and express their ideas through stories.

She has published her first book "The Mysterious Island" which is a short adventure story in 2019 at the age of 8.

The money raised by the sale of this book goes to the charity, Akshaya Patra Foundation UK.

Deeva published her second children's book " Poco 'o' Lombo is Vesuvius " at the age of 10.

Deeva then went on to publish her first novel "The Space Orb" at the age of 11 and all the proceeds from the sale of this book goes to The St. Luke's Hospice.

Deeva was awarded "She Inspires" Award 2019 under the category of Special Mention - Bright Artist by Inspiring Indian Women on "International Women's Day" at the House of Lords.

She has also received the Pride of Brent "Inspirational Young Person" Award in 2019.

The Trustees of Shree Jalaram Mandir, Greenford felicitated her with a shawl for being one of the youngest author.

She was also recognised for her excellent work of writing and publishing children's books by the Mayor of the London Borough of Ealing.

Deeva has been also been awarded this year with the "Young Innovators Creating a Better World for All " Award by Women Economic Forum .

Book is available to be borrowed from :
The British Library
The Brent Libraries
The Ealing Libraries

Book Readings conducted at :
1. The Bhavan
2. Sai School of Harrow
3. Aadishakti UK
4. Friends & Families of Avanti

Acknowledgments

I would like to express my deepest gratitude to the people who have been my pillars of support throughout the journey of writing this book.

First and foremost, to my loving mum and dad, whose unwavering belief in me and boundless encouragement have been my constant source of inspiration. Your love and support have been the foundation upon which this book was built.

To my dedicated publishers, Ekta and Monica, your commitment to this project, your invaluable insights, and your tireless efforts in bringing this book to life have been nothing short of remarkable. I am grateful for the trust you placed in me and the opportunity to work alongside you. A special thank you to the talented author, Sarah Mussi, for your mentorship and guidance. Your expertise and wisdom have been invaluable in shaping the narrative and ensuring this book reached its full potential.

To my dear friends, who have cheered me on, offered their feedback, and provided a shoulder to lean on during the ups and downs of this creative journey, your friendship has been a priceless gift. Thank you for your unwavering support.

Lastly, I extend my thanks to all those whose names may not appear here but have played a part, big or small, in the creation of this book. Your contributions have not gone unnoticed.

This book is a reflection of the collective effort, love, and encouragement I have received, and I am truly grateful to each and every one of you.

RESURGENCE

YOUNG

The "Young Voices" imprint by Author In Me is a unique and inspiring collection of literary works of young minds. Featuring books penned exclusively by children aged between 7 to 14 years old, this imprint offers readers a fresh, unfiltered perspective of the world through the eyes of the youth. These young authors, with their raw talent and untamed passion for storytelling, bring forth tales that range from whimsical fantasies to profound reflections, challenging the conventional norms of literature. "Young Voices" not only provides a platform for budding writers to showcase their talent but also encourages readers of all ages to appreciate the depth and diversity of thoughts that children are capable of expressing. In a world dominated by adult voices, this imprint is a breath of fresh air, reminding us of the wonder, innocence, and brilliance that childhood brings.

RESURGENCE

RESURGENCE